This Book Belongs To:

....

....

Age............................

Written by Beryl Johnston, illustrated by Dorothea King (Linden Artists).

Published by
GRANDREAMS LIMITED
Jadwin House, 205/211 Kentish Town Road,
London NW5 2JU.

Printed in Czechoslovakia

Contents

WOODLAND TALES

The Spring Rainbow

"Hey, Hopper, *do* get up!"

Pixie Hopper rubbed his eyes and hopped out of bed as he heard a squeaky voice outside his tree house and a rapping on his windowpane.

Then THUMP, THUMP, THUMP! there came a banging at the door and another voice called: "Do open the door, Hopper, we've something *important* to tell you!"

"I'm coming," shouted Hopper. He opened the door and two wild looking figures rushed inside. Hetty Hedgehog had just woken from her winter sleep and still had dry leaves sticking to her prickly back. Hotfoot hare had raced through the meadow and was quite out of breath.

"It's springtime! We're *sure* it is. But something's wrong," squeaked Hetty.

"Spring is here and yet it's not here," declared Hotfoot, flopping onto the nearest chair.

"Stop talking in riddles," said Hopper, putting some cornflakes on the table.

"We'll tell you about it while we're having breakfast," said Hetty. "I'm hungry. I haven't had anything to eat since last autumn."

So they all sat round the table, tucking into milk and cornflakes and talking between mouthfuls.

"It's the flowers," said Hotfoot. "They're not out yet!"

"And they should be," interrupted Hetty. "Violets and bluebells and yellow primroses."

Suddenly they heard a clattering sound of footsteps running down the stairs, then Popper and Topper appeared.

Though Hopper liked to live on the ground, so that his friends could call in, Popper spent most of his time in the middle of Tall Ash Tree. There he could look down and see everything that was going on in the glade below.

Topper lived at the top of the tree, because he liked to see right over the other tree tops and talk to the birds as they flew by.

"We came down to see who was making all the noise this morning," they said, helping themselves to cornflakes.

"It was us - me and Hetty," said Hotfoot. "We've just found out that it ought to be springtime."

"But you can't have spring without flowers," explained Hetty.

"Perhaps it needs some rain to make them grow," said Topper, poking his head out of the window. "I can't see much of the sky from down here, but it seems to have gone awfully dark." A large spot of rain fell on his nose and he quickly pulled his head back inside.

There was a flash of lightning and a roll of thunder, and with a frightened squeak, Hetty disappeared under the table. "I don't like thunderstorms," she squealed.

"Now who would *really* know why the flowers haven't started blooming?" asked Hopper.

"The Wise Witch might know," suggested Popper. "One of us could ask her."

"I think *I'd* better not go and see her," said Hotfoot Hare, looking uncomfortable. "She may have guessed it was me who ate some of the best lettuce in her garden."

"I think it had better not be *me*," squeaked Hetty, peeping out from under the tablecloth. "I'm a bit scared she might want me to help her with her spells."

There was another crash of thunder and Hetty disappeared again.

The rain came pelting down and Topper suddenly remembered he'd left his bedroom window wide open. "I'd better go and shut it," he gasped, "or else everything will get soaking wet!" and he raced back upstairs.

In a minute the others heard him calling: "There's something very strange in the sky. Do come up and see it."

So they all climbed up the long flight of winding stairs that led to the top of Tall Ash Tree.

"Look," said Topper, pointing out of the window. "There's a coloured thing up there." They all saw a big archway of colours spreading over the sky.

"Oh, my," gasped Hetty. "Isn't it pretty. There's red and yellow and green . . ."

"And blue and indigo and violet," finished Popper.

"What can it be?" cried Topper, leaning out of the window.

"It's a *rainbow*," laughed Ashly, the Tall Ash Tree, waving his bare branches. "Haven't you seen one before?"

"No," said Topper. "What's it doing in the sky?"

"I don't know," said Popper, "but it seems to be falling into the wood. The rain has stopped now, so let's go and take a closer look."

"Wait for me," panted Hetty, as everyone dashed downstairs again.

Hopper was the first to run outside, where Ashly was still shaking the raindrops from his branches. "Ooh, one went right down my neck!" cried Hopper.

"Pick a toadstool umbrella," laughed Ashly. "It's still very wet in the wood."

So they all stopped to pick a toadstool to use as an umbrella before hurrying off to look for the rainbow.

At last they came to a large, open glade and there, right in the middle was the rainbow, glowing with colours. They moved closer and Hopper pointed to the place where the rainbow's end hung a little way above the grass. "Look," he cried out in surprise. "There are taps on the end of the rainbow."

"So there are," said Popper. "How strange. There's one for each colour. I wonder what they're for?"

"To pour out the colours, of course," said Topper. "Let's find something to use as cups."

Hetty found three old acorn cups hidden in the grass and gave one each to the pixies. Topper turned on the red tap first and some runny red stuff poured into the cup. He sniffed and smiled. "It smells like strawberries," he said.

Then he took a sip. "It tastes like strawberries and raspberries and cherries, all mixed together," he told the others.

Popper tried the orange colour. "This tastes like oranges, only even nicer," he said.

Hopper turned the yellow tap. "This rainbow juice tastes something like bananas," he said, licking his lips.

They went through all the other colours. The green tasted like gooseberries, the blue like plums. The indigo had a damson flavour and the violet tasted like sugared sweets.

"I don't think you ought to drink any more," said Hotfoot. "Your face has gone a very funny colour."

The pixies looked at each other in dismay. Hotfoot was right. Their faces were covered with rainbow-coloured spots. "Oh, dear, I don't feel very well," gasped Hopper. "I think I may have drunk too much rainbow juice."

"Me, too," agreed Topper, sitting down suddenly and holding his tummy.

Popper was rolling on the grass. "Oh, I'm feeling bad," he groaned. "I wish I hadn't started drinking that stuff."

They hadn't noticed just how much colour they had taken until they heard voices crying: "What has happened to our rainbow?"

Looking up, they saw seven beautiful fairies flying round the rainbow. Each one was dressed in a different rainbow colour.

"Oh, dear," spluttered Hopper. "We didn't know the rainbow belonged to anyone."

"What have you been doing?" asked Flame, the Red Fairy.

"We've been drinking the rainbow juice," confessed Topper. "Now we don't feel well."

"No wonder," cried the other fairies. "We made it specially for colouring the spring flowers. It's for painting, not drinking."

"Look at their faces," said Bells, the Blue Fairy. "They look awful."

"It serves them right," declared Mossy, the Green Fairy. "Perhaps that will teach them not to drink anything unless they know what it is."

The pixies began to cry. They didn't like the fairies being cross with them, but most of all they didn't like the way they were feeling.

"Nobody's ever drunk our rainbow before," sighed Golda, the Yellow Fairy. "We'll have to find the Wise Witch and ask if she can help."

"I'll take you to her cottage," offered Hetty, very bravely. So she ran as fast as she could, with Golda fluttering behind her, to the cottage where the Wise Witch lived.

They were only just in time, for the Wise Witch was just going out to start searching for magic herbs. "I can't understand why everything is so late blooming this year," she was telling Tiptoes, her black cat, who was perched on the windowsill.

"Here comes one of the Rainbow Fairies," meowed Tiptoes. "Perhaps she will know what's the matter."

"The pixies have drunk a lot of colour from our Spring Rainbow," said Golda. "Now they are sick and we don't know how to make them better."

"They've probably got colouritis," declared the witch. "I'll have to give them a dose of my strongest medicine," and she took a big bottle off a shelf, and picking up a large spoon, put them both in her basket.

Hetty led the Yellow Fairy and the Wise Witch back
to the glade where the pixies were huddled at the
rainbow's end. They looked very sorry for themselves.

"Open your mouths wide, "ordered the witch, and she
popped a large spoonful of medicine into each pixie's
mouth.

It tasted horrid. It was worse than anything they had
ever swallowed.

"Ugh!" spluttered Hopper.

"Yuk!" groaned Popper.

"Ow!" cried Topper, pulling a face.

But the witch's medicine worked so well they very soon felt better. "I'll never drink anything strange again," declared Hopper.

"Nor me," said Popper.

"Me neither," agreed Hopper.

"I'm glad I didn't try any of the rainbow juice," Hotfoot whispered to Hetty.

"So am I," said Hetty. "But what are the Rainbow Fairies doing now?"

All the fairies were pouring rainbow colours into acorn cups. Then Fairy Flame gave each one a new paint brush.

"Look, the rain has made all the flowers grow," squeaked Hetty excitedly. "But they haven't any colours yet."

"We are just going to colour them," said Golda, fluttering over from the rainbow and starting to paint a primrose pale yellow. "I just hope we shall have enough to colour the whole woodland."

"Can we help?" asked Hopper.
"To show we're truly sorry we nearly
spoilt your rainbow."

"You can if you promise to be
very careful and not spill any rainbow
paint," agreed Fairy Flame.

So this time the pixies filled
their acorn cups and the Red Fairy
gave them each a new paint brush.

Then Hopper, Popper and
Topper began to help the fairies paint
the bluebells, the violets and the
yellow primroses.

As the sun began to shine brightly, the butterflies came out and they needed painting in bright colours, too. The pixies were kept very busy, in fact they had never worked so hard before.

"We'd better make sure Ashly gets lots of new, green leaves," said Hopper. So they climbed into his branches and he was very pleased to have a fine new covering of green leaves.

"Make sure you cover the very tips of my twigs," he chuckled, stretching his branches in the sun.

By the time everyone had finished, the wood looked really cheerful. "It's lovely," squeaked Hetty, as she and Hotfoot ran around admiring all the bright rainbow colours. "Now we've got a proper springtime in the Woodlands after all."

WOODLAND TALES

Pipkin The Shy Pixie

"My saucepan's fallen to pieces," wailed Pixie Pipkin, as his breakfast porridge spilt all over the cooking stove.

"Ho, ho," he heard a voice chuckling from the hollow tree where he lived. "What are you going to do now, Pipkin?"

Pipkin stepped outside his front door and looked up at Old Oaky, who was grinning from branch to branch. "It's all very well for you to laugh," cried Pipkin, stamping his foot. "You *know* I can't buy a new saucepan."

"And why not?" asked Oaky, raising one thick, bark eyebrow.

"Because . . . because . . ." mumbled Pipkin, then he stopped, went very red and hung his head.

"Because you're too shy," said Oaky. Pipkin nodded and looked miserable.

Oaky rustled his leaves in a big sigh and said, more kindly, "I wish I could think of a cure for you, Pipkin. But if you're too shy to go and buy a new saucepan, you'll have to look for a second-hand one."

"Where can I find a second-hand saucepan?" asked Pipkin.

"Just beyond the woodlands is a dump where the woodland gnomes put all the rubbish that silly people dump in our forest. That's where you may find an old saucepan."

Oaky pointed the way with one of his branches and Pipkin hurried away between the long grass and ferns. Suddenly a big black cat leapt across his path and Pipkin nearly jumped out of his skin.

"Oh, Tiptoes, you *did* give me a fright," he gasped. Tiptoes looked at him curiously. "What are you doing out so early, Pipkin?" she purred.

"I'm going to the rubbish dump to look for a saucepan," said Pipkin.

Tiptoes followed him to the edge of the wood. Beyond the trees lay the rubbish dump and Pipkin looked at it in amazement. There were old bedsteads, worn-out car tyres, cracked cups and broken flowerpots.

"I can't see anything small enough to use as a saucepan," frowned Pipkin, as he started searching round the rubbish dump. But at last he found an empty tin can. "If I fix a handle to this, it will do very well," he decided.

As he looked for a piece of metal to make a handle, he suddenly saw something moving in front of him. IT WAS ANOTHER PIXIE.

Pipkin felt so shy he dropped the can and ran off as fast as his legs would carry him. He dived behind one of the broken flowerpots and hid there, his heart going thumpity-thump.

When at last he got his breath back, Pipkin peeped out again. A little way off was another flowerpot and peeping round it was the other pixie.

Pipkin bobbed out of sight again. Then he thought: "That other pixie must be as shy as I am."

So he peeped out from his flowerpot and waved. The other pixie waved at Pipkin at just the same time. "He must want to be friends," thought Pipkin.

Pipkin came out from behind his flowerpot and so did the other pixie. Pipkin drew a deep breath and was about to call to the other pixie, when he heard a loud noise.

It was some gnomes and their lorry arriving with a load of rubbish. Both pixies ran back to their flowerpots. Pipkin hid behind his, trembling, as the lorry came closer and closer. Then a voice called: "Tip it up here, Bill!"

Pipkin looked out just in time to see a whole load of rubbish falling over the place where the other pixie was hiding. "What shall I do?" he cried, as the lorry drove away. "I'll never be able to dig through all that rubbish and rescue the other pixie. I must get help!"

Pipkin rushed away from the dump and dashed along a woodland path, wondering where he could find help. Then he saw the Wise Witch's cottage.

Quite forgetting that he'd never, ever spoken to the Wise Witch before, he banged on her door.

"Who's knocking on my door?" demanded the Wise Witch.

"Please come and help," cried Pipkin, running inside. "My pixie friend's had a load of rubbish tipped over him and I can't move it myself." And he burst into tears.

Just then there came a loud 'meow' and Tiptoes jumped in through the window and onto the witch's shoulder, purring something into her ear.

"Close your eyes, Pipkin," said the witch. "You musn't look while I make some special magic."

"Oh, do hurry," sobbed Pipkin, as he shut his eyes. He kept them tightly closed while the witch moved around the room, chanting some strange words.

"Now you can open your eyes again," said the witch.

Pipkin opened his eyes and there, standing in front of him, was the other pixie. He looked as though *he'd* been crying, too. But then both pixies clapped their hands and ran towards each other.

Suddenly, Pipkin's head hit something hard and he fell back, onto the floor. "Ooh," he cried. "That other pixie *hit* me."

"There was no other pixie," laughed the witch. "You were looking at your own reflection in an old piece of looking glass on the rubbish dump. You didn't know who it was because you've always been too shy to buy a mirror."

Pipkin burst into tears again. "Then I haven't got a friend after all," he sobbed. "You were just teasing me," he cried.

Before the Wise Witch could stop him, he rushed out of her cottage and ran back along the woodland path. He was in such a temper, he didn't see someone else coming towards him in a hurry.

BUMP! Once again Pipkin banged his head against something hard. "Oh," he cried, as he saw another pixie rubbing his own head. "That witch is playing tricks on me again."

"Why did you hit me?" shouted the other pixie, angrily, coming towards Pipkin with his fists up.

They were just going to start fighting when Pipkin thought of something. "Why, you're real," he cried.

"What are you talking about?" asked Popper, the other pixie.

"I thought . . . ho, ho . . . I thought . . . hee, hee, that you were my reflection," giggled Pipkin.

He explained how the witch had tricked him and then Popper started laughing. They giggled so much that tears ran down their faces.

"Wait till the others hear about this," laughed Popper, leading Pipkin into a big glade. In the middle of the glade grew the tall ash tree where Popper lived with Hopper and Topper.

Asleep

Popper told them all about the trick the witch had played on Pipkin and they thought it was very funny. "You were brave, going to see the Wise Witch all by yourself," said Topper.

"What were you doing at the rubbish dump in the first place?" asked Hopper.

"I went to look for a second-hand saucepan," said Pipkin, suddenly remembering that he still hadn't one.

"Why not get a new saucepan from the Woodland Stores?" asked Popper. "Come along, we'll go with you and buy you one as a present."

So off they went, arm in arm, until they came to Big Beechy, the largest tree in the woodlands. Hanging from one branch was a notice with WOODLAND STORES painted on it.

The other pixies led Pipkin through the main entrance, between two big tree roots. "We'll take a shopping trolley, just for fun," said Hopper.

As soon as they got inside the stores they found the whole place was crowded with other pixies doing their early morning shopping. Pipkin had never seen so many pixies before. He didn't know so many lived in the woodlands. To his surprise he found it all very exciting.

Hopper and Topper pushed the trolley with Pipkin and Popper riding on top. They went all round the shop until they came to the shelves of pots and pans.

"What size saucepan do you need?" asked Hopper, picking up a huge one.

"I only need a small one for my breakfast porridge," said Pipkin. He suddenly remembered he hadn't had any breakfast yet and was feeling very hungry.

"Let's buy a big one as well, for when you have visitors," said Hopper.

So they chose a big saucepan and a small one, and then went to the cash desk to pay for them. "Now we'll help you carry them home," said Popper.

Old Oaky's bark mouth dropped open when he saw them coming. "What ever has happened to Pipkin the shy pixie?" he asked.

"He's made some friends at last," said Tiptoes, who was waiting on the doorstep. "The Wise Witch will be pleased!"

She meowed as Pipkin started to open the door. "The Wise Witch is sorry you were so upset by her little joke, so she sent me along with some *real* magic to make up for it."

Tiptoes dropped a small bag of herbs into the big saucepan and said: "Now put it on the stove to boil and see what happens."

So Pipkin started making porridge with the witch's magic herbs. "That smells so good it's making us all feel hungry," said Popper.

At last the porridge was ready and Pipkin poured some into acorn cups for everyone. Then he gave Tiptoes a large saucer of milk.

Popper, Hopper, Topper and Pipkin sat outside, under Oaky's branches, and began their breakfast. The porridge tasted better than anything they had ever eaten before.

"We'll come and have breakfast with you again," said Hopper, as he started his third helping.

"It was very lucky you bumped into Popper," said Topper. "Now we shall be able to have lots of fun together."

"Oh, yes," laughed Pipkin, and he was so pleased to have found some real friends, he quite forgot that he'd ever been such a shy pixie.

WOODLAND TALES

Bigboots and The Midsummer Ball

"My Midsummer Ball is going to be grander than ever this year," the Fairy Queen told Pixie Bigboots, "and as you are the biggest pixie in Woodlands, I want you to take care that everything is arranged properly."

"Very well, Your Majesty, I will do my best," promised Bigboots, feeling very important.

The Queen was in her Throne Room at the Fairy Palace, and as Bigboots turned to go, all the Rainbow Fairies fluttered in, carrying dresses in every colour of the rainbow. "I wonder which colour the Queen will choose to wear at the ball tonight?" they whispered.

Bigboots knew he would have to hurry if everything was to be ready before the moon rose that night. So he rushed past the Palace Guards, down the green hill and through the high hawthorn hedge that grew all round the palace.

"I must find the other pixies in the woodland and get them to help," he said to himself, looking at the big pile of invitations that had to be delivered.

The first pixies he found were Hopper, Popper and Topper, who were playing rounders with Pipkin and Hotfoot Hare. "Stop wasting time and listen to me," ordered Bigboots. "The Fairy Queen has put me in charge of the arrangements for the Midsummer Ball tonight, so I'll expect everyone to help."

He gave them the silver-edged envelopes. "Take these invitations round to all the fairies in the wood," he said. "I'm off to the Brownies' Bakery to make sure all the food will be ready in time."

At the Birch Tree Bakery, the Brownies were very busy. Bron and Bryn were baking all the cakes for the ball. Honey cakes, cream cakes and special chocolate cakes that the fairies liked best of all.

"We're going to need a lot extra tonight," said Bigboots, pulling out his long list. "You must make sure everything's finished in time."

Brownie Bron pulled another batch of cakes out of the oven. "We're working as fast as we can," he grumbled.

Bryn frowned as she put whirls of icing on top. "Don't start eating them now, Bigboots, or we'll never have enough."

"Just see that they're all delivered to the Great Glade before moonrise tonight," ordered Bigboots, stomping out of the bakery. "I'm going to make sure all the tables are ready." Bron and Bryn put out their tongues at him as he marched away. "That pixie's too big for his boots," giggled Silvery Birch.

Bigboots marched on until he reached the place where the ball was to be held. It was the largest and most beautiful glade in all the woodland. Wild roses grew all round the edge and in the middle the grass was smooth and green.

At least, that was how it usually looked. But as he stepped into the glade, Bigboots cried out in dismay. All over the grass lay the biggest collection of rubbish he'd ever seen in the wood. Bits of paper, orange peel, apple cores and lemonade cartons were scattered around. Even worse, all the toadstool seats and tables had been trampled into the ground.

"What's happened?" he gasped.

"You may well ask," chirped a blackbird, perching on a branch close to Bigboots. "Some of those naughty elves that live in the other wood came along the road that runs past the woodland. They stopped to have a picnic in the woods and left all this rubbish lying around."

"What can I do?" wailed Bigboots. "The Fairy Queen will never be able to have a Midsummer's Ball here tonight."

"You'd better go and ask the gnomes to help," said the blackbird. "They spend most of their time keeping the woodland tidy."

So Bigboots rushed away along a woodland path -
and fell over a wheelbarrow full of broken twigs, fallen
petals and feathers the birds had dropped.

"Hey, watch where you're going," shouted Nudge
the Gnome. "I'm trying to make the place tidy!"

"Then you'd better tidy up the glade," snapped
Bigboots, crossly. "The Fairy Queen wants to hold the
Midsummer Ball there tonight, but it's in a dreadful mess."

"I'd better get some help," said Nudge, and putting two fingers in his mouth, he sent a shrill whistle echoing through the woods.

There was a pattering sound as dozens of feet ran along the woodland paths towards him. Then more gnomes appeared with wheelbarrows and litter bins, and they all began clearing up the Great Glade.

"I don't know where I'm going to find toadstool seats and tables," sighed Bigboots. "I'll have to ask the Wise Witch to help me."

Bigboots hurried away through the woods, until he came to the cottage where the Wise Witch lived. Banging on the door he called: "Wise Witch, are you at home?"

"Who's making such a din on my door?" demanded the Wise Witch, as she flung it open. "Oh, it's you, Bigboots. "What is so important that you have to bring me from my spell-making today?"

"The Fairy Queen is holding her Midsummer Ball tonight, in the Great Glade in the middle of Woodlands. But there won't be enough toadstool seats and tables. How can I get more to grow by tonight?"

"I'll see if I can help," said the witch as Bigboots followed her into the cottage. The room was full of smoke and Tiptoes, the witch's black cat, was sitting on a chair, looking at a big book of magic spells.

The witch went to a cupboard and pulled out a bowl of strange smelling powder. She put some in a bag and handed it to Bigboots. "Scatter this special powder round the edge of the glade and then the toadstools will grow by moonrise," she promised.

On his way back to the glade, Bigboots ran this way and that, along pebble paths and over grassy banks, making sure there wasn't a fallen leaf or dandelion seed floating around. Then, just as he thought everything was spick and span, he caught sight of something in a bush, high above him. It was large and round and gleaming white.

"It's the moon!" gasped Bigboots. "Whatever is it doing down here in the woodland?"

Looking closer, he saw that the 'moon' had a long piece of string tied to it, and this was caught round a branch. "What shall I do?" gasped Bigboots. "Unless I can get it back into the sky there will be no moonlight for the fairies to dance by at the ball tonight."

Stretching up as high as he could, Bigboots was just able to reach the string and pull it free. Then the 'moon', which was really a balloon that had drifted into the wood, began to rise up through the trees.

"Oh, good, it's nearly reached the sky now," cried Bigboots.

Then he cried out in dismay as two magpies hopped out of their nest to take a closer look.

"What is it?" chattered one, flapping his wings in alarm.

"It's a monster," declared the other, and he moved towards the balloon. They both gave a sharp peck with their beaks and BANG! the balloon was no more.

"Oh, you've burst the moon," Bigboots shouted angrily. "Now there'll be no light for the ball tonight and the Fairy Queen will be cross with me," and he burst into tears.

Bigboots ran, sobbing, back to the glade. There everything was neat and tidy, for the gnomes had cleared away all the rubbish and they were rolling the grass to make it smooth for the dancers.

"Oh, what shall we do?" cried Bigboots. "The magpies have burst the moon and there will be no light for the ball tonight." The wood was already becoming dark, for the sun had started to set.

"Perhaps I can help," said a small voice, and looking round, Bigboots saw a small glow-worm sitting on a twig. "If you can find something to use as lanterns, all the glow-worms in Woodlands could give enough light to brighten up the glade."

"I've been sweeping up fallen flowerheads from the foxgloves," said Nudge the Gnome, showing Bigboots his loaded barrow. "If we fix them to the top of these long twigs they will make very good lanterns."

So Bigboots and the gnomes tied the flowerheads to the twigs and stuck them all round the glade. The glow-worms took their places and each became a light for a foxglove lantern.

Then Bigboots remembered the witch's magic powder and sprinkled it all round the edge of the glade, under the lanterns. "I do hope this works in time," he frowned. "The witch said the toadstools would grow by moonrise, but without the moon, how can I tell when that will be?"

As soon as the sun had set, toadstools began to spring up all round the glade. There were small ones to sit on and bigger ones to use as tables.

The last ones had just pushed up out of the ground as Bryn and Bron, the Brownies, came into the glade carrying big trays of cakes from the bakery. Behind them came Hopper, Popper and Topper, with lots of other pixies, all carrying cakes and ice creams and special fizzy drinks for everyone to enjoy.

As they spread everything on the tables, the grasshopper band arrived and the nightingale who had been specially invited to sing at the ball.

Then they heard the pattering of feet along the path that led from the Palace. "It's the Fairy Queen," everyone cried, as a coach pulled by woodmice swept into the glade.

Just as the Fairy Queen stepped from her coach, something round and gleaming white rose in the sky and sent silvery beams into the middle of the glade.

"It's the moon," cried Bigboots. "But I thought it had burst! "

The Fairy Queen smiled and called Bigboots to her side. "How well you have arranged everything for the ball, Bigboots," she said.

"It wasn't just me, Your Majesty," Bigboots told her. "Everyone in the woodland helped to get everything ready in time."

"And who thought of the fairy-lights?" asked the Queen.

"The glow-worms," said Bigboots, and he explained how he thought the moon had burst.

"How clever to have made all these lanterns," laughed the Queen. "They make the glade look prettier than ever." Then she made a speech telling all the fairies how lucky they were that the ball had not been spoilt.

They all cheered the pixies, the Brownies, the Wise Witch, the gnomes and the glow-worms. They then gave a special cheer for Bigboots.

"Perhaps Bigboots isn't so bad after all," said Pixie Popper.

"No," agreed Brownie Bryn. "I'll give him some of our nicest cakes."

So the music played and the fairies danced, and everyone said it was the best Midsummer Ball they'd ever known.

"It is a lovely ball," agreed Bigboots, "and everyone was even more helpful when I didn't order them around. So I don't think I'll ever try to be bossy again!"

WOODLAND TALES

Bushy Tail's Bedtime

"Don't go too far, now, Bushytail," warned Mrs Squirrel, her arms full of acorns. "It's nearly bedtime."

"It can't be," Bushytail called back. "The sun's still shining brightly."

"It's going to get very cold quite soon," said his mother. "I can smell winter in the air. When Jack Frost comes you'll need to be warmly tucked up in bed."

"I don't believe it," chuckled Bushytail to himself, as he flicked his long, bushytail and ran away from his tree-top house. "It's as warm as summer," and he leapt from branch to branch, shaking off the gold and red autumn leaves.

Ossie Owl saw him coming and hopped out of his house in Old Oak. "Don't go too far, Bushytail," he called. "It's getting colder and if you stay out too late you'll get frost in your tail."

"I wish they'd stop teasing me," said Bushytail. "It's a lovely day. The woodlands are much brighter than ever I've known them."

He was right, because lots of leaves had already fallen so that the sunlight seemed to fill even the dark places in the wood. He dropped to the ground and snuffled through the leaves for ripe nuts.

Then he heard a crunch, crunch, CRUNCH! over the leaves and he sprang behind a tree stump.

It was Bigboots, the pixie. "Oh, Bigboots, you did give me a fright," said Bushytail, as Bigboots stopped to gather more nuts into the big sack he was carrying. "And why are you collecting so many nuts? You can't eat them all at once."

"I'll need them for the winter," said Bigboots. "Soon it will be cold and frosty and there will be no nuts to eat unless I store them in the larder."

"But it's so warm," said Bushytail. "I'm sure summer will soon be here again," and he hurried away.

Soon he reached Tall Ash Tree and stopped to watch the three pixies who lived in the tall tree. Hopper was sweeping leaves from his doorway while Popper and Topper were taking down a hammock from the branches.

"Why are you doing that?" asked Bushytail.

"Because it will soon be winter and then it will be too cold to stay outside for long," said Topper.

Hetty Hedgehog popped out of her home under the tree roots and grabbed an armful of the leaves that Hopper had swept into a heap. "These will make a lovely warm lining for my bedroom," she said.

Bushytail looked puzzled. "It's so warm and sunny," he said. "I'm sure summer will soon he here again."

"No, not for a long time," laughed Hopper. "You've only seen one summer, Bushytail, and this is your first autumn. You can't *think* what winter will be like."

"I don't know and I don't care," replied Bushytail, flicking his long tail. "I'm off to see if the walnuts are ripe," and he scampered away through the trees.

At the very edge of the wood, Bushytail stopped. In front of him he could see a large meadow where the sun was shining even more brightly.

Some fieldmice were busy collecting large red rosehips that hung from the bushes. Bushytail liked hips, too, but he was looking for something he liked even better. Then he saw, far away on the other side of the meadow, a big walnut tree.

Bushytail went leaping across the grass towards the circle of yellow leaves that already lay under Wally Walnut's wide-spreading branches.

"Can I have some of your nuts, please, Wally?" he asked, sitting on his hind legs and looking up at the big tree.

"If you can find any," sighed Wally. "The rooks have been feasting on them since long before they were ripe. You can run up my trunk and have a look, but please don't tickle my nose with your tail!"

"I can't see many nuts here," squeaked Bushytail, leaping about the branches and sending more leaves falling to the ground.

"I'm not surprised," yawned Wally Walnut, stretching his branches until they creaked. "It's getting on for winter, you know. There's bound to be a frost tonight, I can feel it in my twigs - they're starting to tingle."

"Everybody keeps talking about the frost. But what is it like?" asked Bushytail.

"You'll see for yourself, soon enough," sighed Wally. "But it's high time you were going back home. You don't want to be caught out here when Jack Frost comes along."

"Pooh," said Bushytail. "I'm sure it can't be that bad. Anyway, I've just found some ripe nuts." He was feeling really hungry and started nibbling them as fast as he could. "They're very tasty," he told Wally, his mouth full.

He was so busy nibbling, he didn't notice the sun getting lower in the sky. But suddenly the rooks started squabbling and rose, squawking into the air. As they flew off, Bushytail saw the long shadows falling over the meadow and shivered.

"Perhaps I'd b...better be getting back to the wood, or I might not be able to find my way home in the dark," he admitted, and quickly ran back down the trunk. "Goodnight, Wally. Thanks for the nuts."

"Goodnight, Bushytail."

Bushytail began to make his way back across the meadow. As he got near the bushes where he'd first seen the fieldmice, they all came dashing past him. "Hurry home, Bushytail, Jack Frost's coming!" they squeaked.

By now it had become so dark that Bushytail could hardly see his way across the meadow. As he ran this way and that, trying to find his way amongst the hillocks, the moon slowly rose in the sky. By its pale light, Bushytail saw a strange figure coming towards him.

It was Jack Frost. He was scattering frost all over the grass, making it gleam in the moonlight. As Jack hurried past him, a big handful of hoare frost fell over the little squirrel's tail.

"Ooh, my tail's so cold it's gone all numb," squeaked Bushytail, shivering. "I can't move it!"

"Ho, ho," laughed Jack Frost, looking round at
Bushytail. "You do look funny. This is the first time I've
caught a squirrel by putting frost on his tail."

"It's not funny," sobbed Bushytail. He needed his tail to
help him keep his balance as he ran through the grass. But
now it was so stiff, he couldn't move.

"What shall I do?" he squeaked, as Jack Frost went on
his way. "I'll never get home, now. I'm so c...c...cold. I wish
I'd listened to the pixies' warning. But they'll all be in bed
now and nobody will come and find me."

But not all the Woodlanders were in bed, in fact, at that moment one had just come out of the wood and was flying over the meadow. Suddenly Bushytail saw a dark shape gliding through the air above him. It fluttered down and landed on a frosty tree stump.

"What kind of trouble are you in *now*, Bushytail?" asked Ossie Owl. "Your tail is all sparkling."

"Jack Frost threw this white stuff over it and made it go stiff," cried Bushytail. "Now I can't move. I'm so c...c...cold," he said, his teeth chattering.

"Hmm. There's not much I can do on my own," said Ossie. "I'd better get some help." He swooped off, back to the wood, leaving Bushytail sparkling and shivering in the moonlight.

"Young Bushytail's in a fix," hooted Ossie, as he landed close to High Ash Tree. The three pixies were just coming out with their glow-worm lanterns.

"Mrs Squirrel told us he was missing, so we were going to start searching for him," said Hopper.

"He's in the middle of the meadow, frozen stiff," said Ossie. "He can't move because Jack Frost put frost on his tail. I don't know how we're going to rescue him."

"I know just what we need," said Popper, rushing back into the tree-house.

It was not long before Bushytail saw Hopper, Popper and Topper coming towards him, with Ossie showing them the way. "There he is," called Ossie. "Turn right by that big thistle and you'll find him behind the next hillock."

"Bushytail!" called Topper. "All the Woodlanders are searching for you. We didn't think of looking in the meadow."

The pixies had brought the large net hammock. They spread it on the ground and rolled Bushytail into it.

Then, with Hopper leading the way and Ossie flying overhead, they marched back to the woods.

"How are we going to thaw out Bushytail?" asked Popper, as they carried him along, under the trees.

"That's going to be a hard job," said Hopper. Then he sniffed the air. "I can smell something cooking."

Through the trees they saw the glow of a fire and as they got closer, they saw Bigboots outside his house, roasting chestnuts.

"What *have* you got there?" called Bigboots, when he saw the pixies with their hammock.

"A squirrel with frost in his tail," Popper told him.

"Then you'd better thaw him out by my fire," said Bigboots.

The pixies put down their load and Bigboots came over to look. "*Bushytail*, I might have guessed it was you!" declared Bigboots, helping to lift him from the hammock and standing him with his back to the fire. "This will soon thaw out your tail."

Bigboots put a hot chestnut between Bushytail's front paws and as he nibbled it, he felt the warmth running down into his toes and right through his tail.

The frost melted away and steamed into the air, until Bushytail could feel his tail again and flick it from side to side.

"Oh, thank you, Bigboots," he cried. "I feel much better now. Could I have just one more roast chestnut, then I'm sure I shall feel quite better again?"

Bigboots took down one of his big socks from the washing line and Hopper helped fill it with hot chestnuts. "Now we'll take you home to bed," they told Bushytail.

"Bushytail, where have you been?" cried Mrs Squirrel, as they all came back to his tree-top home. "You should have been in bed hours ago!"

"I went off to the meadow and got frost in my tail," confessed Bushytail. "I didn't believe what everybody told me about the cold weather, but now I've felt it and I don't like it."

Before Mrs Squirrel tucked up Bushytail, the pixies put the sock of hot chestnuts in his bed, to keep him warm.

"That's much better," he said, snuggling against it and curling his tail around himself. "When I wake up I can nibble some of the nuts, so I won't have to go out in the cold."

The pixies crept out of the room and Ossie peeped through the window. "Goodnight, Bushytail," he hooted. But Bushytail was already fast asleep.